儿童情绪管理与性格培养

WE ARE ALL GOOD FRIENDS

我们都是好朋友

胡媛媛 编

广东旅游出版社
GUANGDONG TRAVEL & TOURISM PRESS
中国·广州

图书在版编目（ＣＩＰ）数据

我们都是好朋友 / 胡媛媛编. — 广州：广东旅游出版社，2016.11
（儿童情绪管理与性格培养绘本）
ISBN 978-7-5570-0551-1

Ⅰ.①我… Ⅱ.①胡… Ⅲ.①儿童故事－图画故事－中国－当代 Ⅳ.①I287.8

中国版本图书馆 CIP 数据核字(2016)第 237811 号

总 策 划：罗艳辉
责任编辑：殷如筠
封面绘图：赵里骏
责任技编：刘振华
责任校对：李瑞苑

我 们 都 是 好 朋 友
WOMEN DOU SHI HAO PENGYOU

广东旅游出版社出版发行

（广州市越秀区建设街道环市东路 338 号银政大厦西楼 12 楼　　邮编：510030）
邮购电话：020-87348243
广东旅游出版社图书网
www.tourpress.cn
湖北楚天传媒印务有限责任公司
（湖北省武汉市东湖新技术开发区流芳园横路 1 号　邮编：430205）
787 毫米 × 1092 毫米　16 开　2 印张　1 千字
2016 年 11 月第 1 版第 1 次印刷
定价：15.00 元

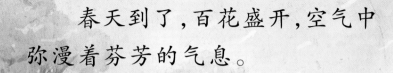

春天到了，百花盛开，空气中弥漫着芬芳的气息。

Spring had come. Flowers were blooming in a riot of color. Fragrance of the blossoms filled the air.

小伙伴们唱着歌儿，排着队伍高高兴兴地去春游。

Kids were singing and queued up for the spring tour.

走在最前面的小鸭子不小心掉进了路边的大坑里,他连忙大喊:"救命啊! 救命啊!"

Duckling was in front of the queue and fell into a pit incautiously. "Help, help!" shouted Duckling.

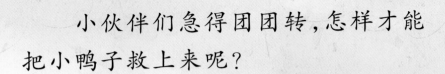

小伙伴们急得团团转，怎样才能把小鸭子救上来呢？

Kids were very anxious. How could they help Duckling?

大象将自己长长的鼻子伸进大坑，说："小鸭子，快抓住我的鼻子。"

Elephant reached out with his trun into the pit and said, "Duckling, hold m trunk!"

8

但是，无论怎么努力，小鸭子还
是够不到大象的鼻子。

But no matter how hard Duckling tried,
he couldn't reach the trunk.

小猴连忙说：
"你的办法不行，还
是让我来吧！"只
见他拿起一根树枝，
爬到树上，倒挂着
把树枝伸进坑里。

"That doesn't work, let me do this!"
said Monkey. He picked up a branch
and climbed up a tree; he hanged upside
down and then reached out the branch
into the pit.

小鸭子跳了跳，
依然够不着树枝。

Duckling tried to reach to the branch, but he failed.

15

小兔急中生智，想到了一个好办法：他提来满满一桶水，倒进大坑。这时，大伙都明白了小兔的办法——把坑里灌满水，小鸭子就可以自己游上来了！

A good idea occurred to Rabbit's mind.
He carried a pail of water and then filled the
pit with the water. By now, everyone got
Rabbit's idea. By filling the pit with water,
Duckling can swim to the ground!

可是坑太大了，一桶水远远不够，大象说："我们再去河边盛水吧！"

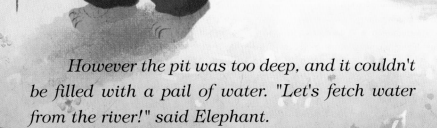

However the pit was too deep, and it couldn't be filled with a pail of water. "Let's fetch water from the river!" said Elephant.

不一会儿，大象吸了满满一鼻子水，小兔和小猴也各自端水来到大坑旁。

In no time, Elephant sopped a lot of water with his trunk. Rabbit and Monkey also returned to the pit with much water.

"哗啦啦"，他们把水都倒进了大坑里。

Walla-walla. They poured the water into the pit.

23

大坑中的水满了，小鸭子浮了上来，他轻轻一跃，跳出了大坑。

The pit was filled and Duckling came up.
He jumped out to the pit with ease.

小鸭子感激地说："真是太谢谢你们了！"

"Thank you so much!" said Duckling.

"不用谢，我们都是好朋友！"说完，大家又快快乐乐地去春游了。

"You are welcome! We are good friends!"
They continued the spring tour happily.

给父母的话：

　　对孩子来说，朋友是十分重要的，朋友是他学习生活中的好伙伴，是他分享快乐悲伤的知心人，真挚的友谊对于孩子的健康成长起着举足轻重的作用。

　　然而，人生离不开友谊，但要得到真正的友谊才是不容易。友谊总需要忠诚去播种，用热情去灌溉，用原则去培养，用谅解去维护。孩子在与朋友的交往中往往容易走入歧途，有的言谈不慎，使朋友的自尊心受到损伤；有的喜欢强人所难，使朋友感到左右为难；有的随意反悔，使朋友感到你不可信赖……诸如此类，都是孩子在与朋友交往时容易走入的误区。

　　作为孩子表率和榜样的家长应该对孩子加以引导，让孩子树立正确的交友观，要让孩子认识到，朋友之间贵在相知相助，就像故事中的小鸭子掉进了坑里，它的好朋友大象、小兔等想方设法营救它一样，这才是真正的好朋友应该做到的。

　　另外，家长还应该让孩子意识到，朋友并非越多越好，应该多交几个志同道合的朋友，当孩子遇到困难时，能支持孩子；当孩子遭遇挫折时，能激励孩子；当孩子陷入迷茫时，能指引孩子；当孩子面对挑战时，能成就孩子。